The Day the Daisies Danced

by **Dee Lillegard**

pictures by **Rex Barron**

G. P. Putnam's Sons   New York

G. P. Putnam's Sons, a division of The Putnam & Grosset Group,
200 Madison Avenue, New York, NY 10016.
G. P. Putnam's Sons, Reg. U.S. Pat. & Tm. Off.
Published simultaneously in Canada.
Printed in Hong Kong by South China Printing Company (1988) Ltd.
Book designed by Patrick Collins.
Text set in Bell.

Library of Congress Cataloging-in-Publication Data
Lillegard, Dee.   The day the daisies danced / by Dee Lillegard;
pictures by Rex Barron.   p.   cm.
Summary: Daisies, tulips, and other flowers celebrate the wedding
of Columbine and Sweet William.
[1. Flowers—Fiction. 2. Weddings—Fiction. 3. Stories in rhyme.]
I. Barron, Rex, ill. II. Title.
PZ8.3.L6144Day   1996   [E]—dc20   93-30583 CIP AC
ISBN 0-399-22661-3

1 3 5 7 9 10 8 6 4 2

First Impression

For Camellia–D.L.

For Ralph Vaughan Williams
and C.G. Jung–R.B.

On the day the daisies danced,
the roses rose from their garden bed.
The buttercups called out for bread,
and the tulips opened up and said,
"Give us a kiss, Camellia."

So…shy Camellia came, tip-toe,
and kissed them.

On the day the daisies danced,
Camellia chanced to overhear
a very tender balladeer.
"Oh, my darling Columbine,"
sang Sweet William, "please be mine!"

And Columbine replied, "I will,
my sweet Sweet William, my Sweet Bill."
The morning glories winked a wink…
"They'll be so happy, don't you think?"
Camellia's cheeks turned tickled pink,
and the daisies danced.

From the morning glories, the word soon spread.
"A wedding! A wedding! They're going to wed!"

"Oh, forget me not," the forget-me-not said.

"Come one, come all!" the trumpets blared.
"Everyone's invited," William declared.

Camellia, excited, clapped her hands,
and the daisies danced.

The violets arrived in their best blue shawls,
and the daffodils dressed in overalls.
Tiger Lily wore her smooth, striped coat,
and Water Lily came in a pea-green boat.

The petunias, the pansies, and a passion flower
rushed in a flurry to the wedding bower.

The phlox milled around in a sheepish crowd.
The red rose read a poem aloud.

"There isn't a cloud in the sky," said Camellia.
And the daisies danced.

Then the bright-eyed bride and groom appeared—
and the garden sage, with his scarlet beard.

And as the sunflower rose to shine,
the sage helped William and Columbine
tie the knot with honeysuckle vine.

They said *I do* that afternoon,
and kissed—and made the tulips swoon
and Camellia smile.
And the daisies danced,
danced all the while.

The bluebells rang, *dingdong, dingdong.*
The tulips sang a wedding song.

Then the trumpet flowers blew their horns,
and the roses strummed their strings with thorns.

The dandelion roared, "Heigh-ho! Heigh-ho!"
and *everybody* danced—some fast, some slow.

Around and around Camellia whirled.
Around and around Camellia twirled
with the daisies, dancing, dancing
until…

The music stopped, and one by one,
the flowers drooped and sighed, "Well done."

The violets shrank
and the sunflower sank
down, down the sky.

And the day's eyes closed,
and the daisies dozed.
Who would ever have supposed
that they could kick their heels so high?

Camellia, shy Camellia.